This book belongs to:

PEARLY ON A PILLOW

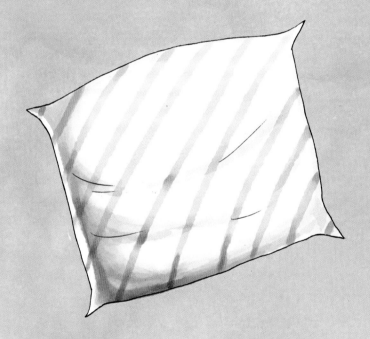

Story by Laura Pricer
Art by Jen Beaudoin

Mountainside Press

The day has come, your tooth is loose!
Your pearly white, it's of no more use.

Jiggle it, wiggle it, to set it free.
When it finally comes out,
how happy you'll be!

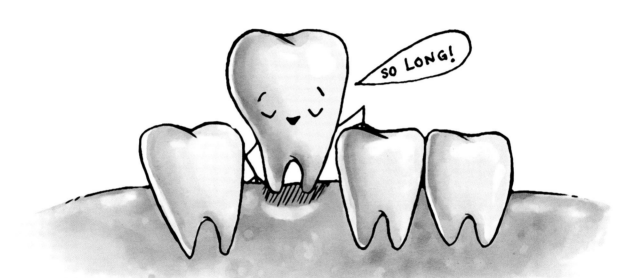

This is the moment, it's all in the wrist.
Close your eyes, grab tight and give it a twist.

Give it a pull ~ hip, hip hooray!
Your pearly white tooth came out, straightaway!

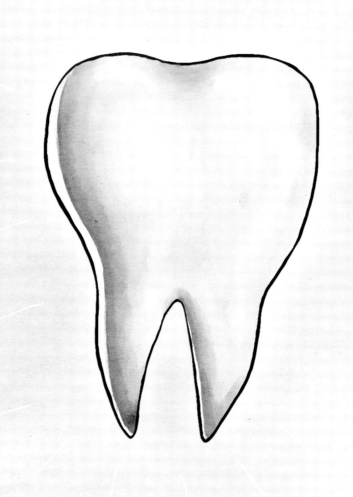

Now what to do? Your tooth is a prize.
Tonight is the night the Tooth Fairy flies.

A couple of quarters, a dollar or two,
A reward will be given to the brave one, that's you!

Now here is a secret, so each of you know.
There's a friend Fairy sends to battle each foe.

Dust bunnies, bed monsters - oh, what a fright!
May take that prize tooth, for their own in the night.

Fairy's friend is named Pearly, like your pearly white.
He'll hold tight to your tooth, keep it safe—out of sight.

No dust bunnies or monsters will steal your prize tooth
You'll get your reward and that is the truth!

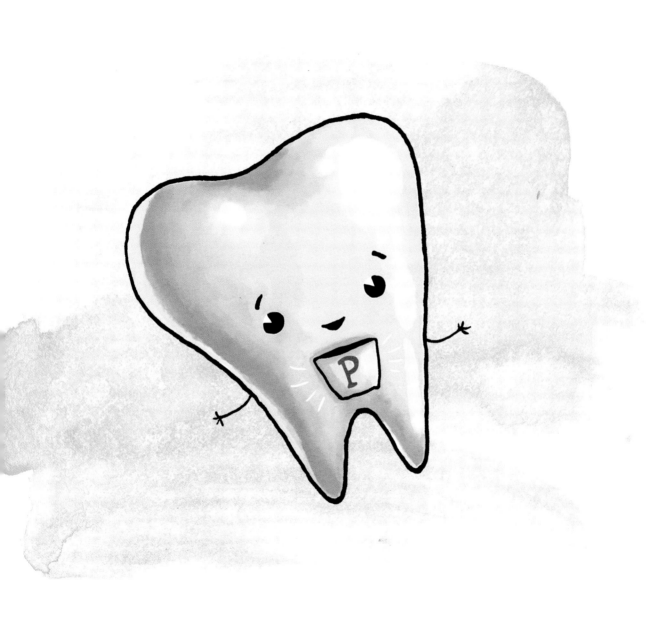

Hide your tooth in his pouch,
then a rule you must follow.
Pearly's placed on his pillow, until it's tomorrow.

His pillow's the place your tooth also stays
'Til Fairy can get there and whisk it away.

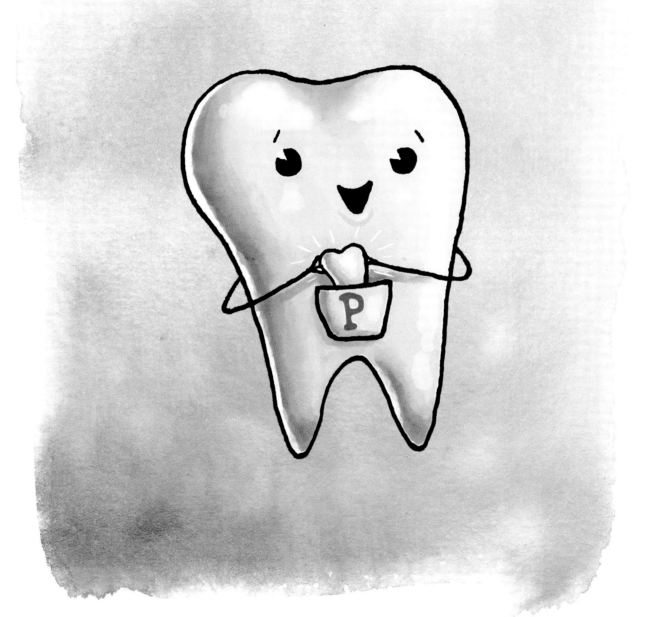

Gently with care, Pearly hands her your tooth.
Tooth Fairy will take it, with a ping and a poof!

A reward will be left in a place warm and fuzzy.
She'll choose Pearly's pouch, it's right on his tummy!

Wake in the morning, get the prize that she left!
You'll be oh, so happy, there'll be no regret.

Pearly's job will be done, till your next tooth comes out
Then he'll keep that one safe like the others, no doubt!

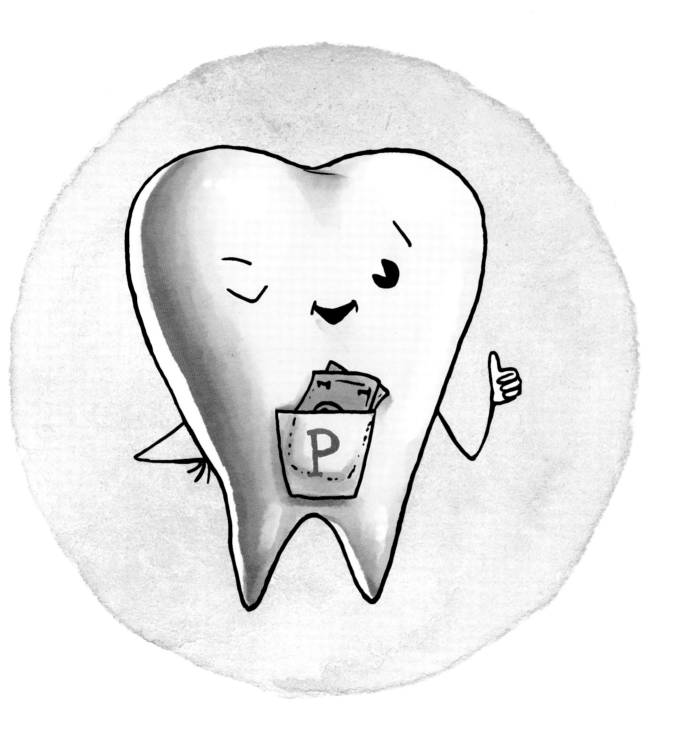

Your Very Own
Pearly Tooth Log

_____'s first tooth came out
on _____.

(Place your photos or draw your tooth in the spaces provided)

Second tooth came out on

_____

Third tooth came out on

_____

Fourth tooth came out on

Fifth tooth came out on

_____

Sixth tooth came out on

_____

Tooth Gallery!

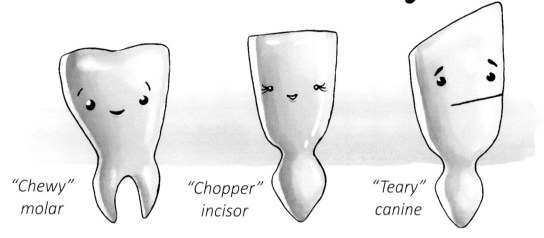

"Chewy"
molar

"Chopper"
incisor

"Teary"
canine

Copyright © 2017 by Laura Pricer
Illustrated by Jen Beaudoin,
Color Work by Matt Beaudoin, Book Design by Lori Taylor
ISBN: 978-0-692-99774-1

Published in the U.S.A., 2018
Mountainside Press, MI
www.pearlyonapillow.com
Printed in the U.S.A. by
Signature Book Printing
www.sbpbooks.com